To Bethany and Luke

Six Foot Six

Kit de Waal

PENGUIN BOOKS

PENGUIN BOOKS

UK | USA | Canada | Ireland | Australia
India | New Zealand | South Africa

Penguin Books is part of the Penguin Random House group of companies
whose addresses can be found at global.penguinrandomhouse.com.

First published in Penguin Books 2018
001

Copyright © Kit de Waal, 2018

The moral right of the author has been asserted

Set in 12/16 pt Stone Serif
Typeset by Jouve (UK), Milton Keynes
Printed in Great Britain by Clays Ltd, St Ives plc

A CIP catalogue record for this book is available from the British Library

ISBN: 978–0–241–31792–1

www.greenpenguin.co.uk

MIX
Paper from
responsible sources
FSC® C018179

Penguin Random House is committed to a
sustainable future for our business, our readers
and our planet. This book is made from Forest
Stewardship Council® certified paper.

Chapter One

Timothy Flowers stands at the corner of Gas Street and Yew Tree Lane. It's the third of November and it's Friday and it's fifteen minutes past eleven o'clock in the morning. In a few minutes, Timothy will see the number forty-five bus. It will be the new Enviro 400 City Bus with the back-to-front design. It's electric. You can get the internet on the new Enviro 400.

Timothy has seen the new bus before. Once. It was so quiet that he didn't even know it was coming and he wasn't ready for it. It went past before Timothy could have a proper look, so this time he is waiting at the bottom of the hill. It's an exciting day for two reasons. First of all, it's Timothy's birthday. His mum said he was nearly born the next day so, just before midnight, Timothy will be twenty-one years old. Secondly, he will see the new Enviro 400 City Bus and there are only fourteen of them in the whole of the city.

'Oi, mate!'

Timothy turns and sees a man in the front

yard of the first house nearest the corner. The house isn't like Timothy's house. Timothy's house has double glazing that keeps out all the noise from the street so Timothy can sleep at night. Timothy's mum says that sometimes, when his brain hasn't had enough rest, Timothy gets confused, so she makes sure he goes to bed by nine o'clock. Then she checks on him after *News at Ten*. But the house at the corner has windows missing at the top and the bottom. The windows at the side are made of pretty coloured glass in green and yellow and red. The house used to be all boarded up, but someone is making it nice again. It's old and tall with a big basement. The basement has a small front yard below street level which is very dirty and untidy. It's as untidy as the man who is standing in it without a shirt on shouting 'Oi, mate!' all the time.

The man must be freezing. He has dirt on his naked chest and stripes of muck on his cheeks like war paint. He has black hair that is oily and curly and one big blob of black dirt under his nose that looks like a moustache. If he was in a film, he would be Charlie Chaplin. Charlie Chaplin films are the best because they're funny and sad at the same time. But Timothy's mum says silent films are the best because they give her peace and quiet.

As well as shouting, the man is pointing at Timothy and waving. 'Yes, you!' he says. 'You! The longfella! Here, down here!'

If there's one thing that Timothy has been told over and over again, it's never ever talk to strangers. So Timothy turns away to look up the road in case the bus is coming.

'Oi, kid!' shouts the man again. 'Here, Long-fella, listen! Come here!'

The man is smiling and beckoning Timothy over with his hand. 'Come here a minute! Stand a bit closer so I don't have to shout.'

Timothy walks to the edge of the sunken yard and leans over the wall so he can see all of the man instead of just his top half. The man has proper muscles on his chest and arms, and a chain with a cross on it round his neck.

'Listen, I'm in need of a favour,' he says. Even though it's really cold, the man is sweating and he wipes his forehead with the back of his hand.

'You talk funny,' says Timothy.

'Well, I can't help that,' says the man. 'I'm from Dublin. You're a local lad, are you, from around here?'

'Yes.'

'And you're off somewhere? Only you've been at that corner for ten minutes. What are you waiting for? And don't say a bus because there's no bus stop as far as I can see.'

'The bus stop is at the next corner,' says Timothy and points up the road. 'You go up the hill, and then at the top you'll see Grove Road and the bus stop is by the Pound Shop. It's got a shelter and an electric sign that tells you the minutes you have to wait.'

'No, listen,' says the man. 'I don't want to know where the bus stop is, no. Listen, what I'm asking is this. Are you doing anything right now? I mean, if you're just standing around, I've got a proposition for you.'

'Proposition?'

'Hold on there now, Longfella,' says the man, 'I'm putting a right strain on my neck looking up at you.'

The man climbs back into the basement window and comes straight out again with a very white shirt and a dirty towel. He climbs up the ladder that leads from the basement yard to the street, hops over the wall and stands in front of Timothy.

'Christ,' he says. 'I seen you walk up to that corner and I thought there's the answer to my

4

bloody prayers, right there. What are you, six foot six?'

Timothy looks down at the man. 'I am six foot five plus seven-eighths of an inch, but that's when I've got no shoes on. When I'm wearing these shoes,' says Timothy, and he holds one foot up so the man can see the sole, 'I am bigger than six foot six inches. I'm six foot six and a half. I've got a different pair of shoes at home, and when I wear them I'm only six foot six and a quarter. I'm twenty-one today. It's my birthday. And my mum says people shouldn't swear.'

All the time Timothy is speaking, the man is wiping his face and his chest with the dirty towel. 'Your mam, eh? Right. Yes. Well, she's right. No swearing. Where was I? All right, listen now. What are you doing today? I mean right now. What are you doing standing at that corner? You look to me like a lad that's come out of the house because he's a bit bored. Because if you are, and you're not busy or doing anything else, you could help me out.'

'How?' says Timothy.

Even though he is still dirty, the man puts his very white shirt on and buttons it up. He has forgotten the black mark under his nose and Timothy points to it.

'You look like Charlie Chaplin, you do.'

'Funny you should say that,' says the man, tucking his shirt into his black trousers and tightening the belt, 'because that's what they call me. Charlie. I'm Colin really – Colin Charles Pearson – but Charlie stuck on account of the fact that Colin makes me sound like a right plank.' He holds his hand out for Timothy to shake, but all the time he is looking up and down.

'Christ,' he says, 'you're as big as a wardrobe and no mistake. What do I call you?'

'Timothy Flowers.'

'Blimey. Really? Flowers?'

'Timothy Joseph Flowers.'

'Okay, Flowers, it's like this.'

'Yes?'

'Here's my situation. I've been let down. I own that house there and I'm repairing it, you know, bringing it up to scratch. Big job. Very big job. Very important job. Time sensitive. It matters a lot. And I had a couple of blokes coming to take up the concrete in that basement and they've not turned up. They've let me down. I only came to open up, and instead I've been at it for three hours solid. Knackered, I am. Half past eight, I said. Half feckin' eight.'

Charlie's voice has been getting louder and

louder. All of a sudden he looks up the road and down the road just in case the late blokes have decided to come after all. Then Charlie says something quickly that sounds like he's still swearing, but much quieter and maybe in Irish. Then he looks at Timothy and claps his hands.

'And so that's where you come in, Longfella, mate. Like I say, you could be the answer to my prayers or, at the very least, get me temporarily out of the bloody shite – sorry, I mean to say, the difficulties in which I find myself.'

'How?'

'Well,' says Charlie, pointing at Timothy's chest. 'You've got something I need, something I haven't got. I need either two normal-sized men, like me, or –' Charlie reaches up and slaps Timothy on his shoulder – 'one of you. See, you, lad, are, like I said, a wardrobe and a double wardrobe at that. Me, I'm more your IKEA bookcase.'

'Why do you need a wardrobe?'

'No, I don't.' Charlie looks up at the sky and takes a very deep breath. Then he looks at his watch and shakes his head. 'Time's ticking on. How to put this? You're like, say, Batman, big and strong, and I'm just Robin, smaller by a good nine inches. I'm Luke Skywalker and you are Chewbacca.'

Timothy shakes his head. 'Chewbacca is seven foot six inches. It says so in my book.'

'Yeah, but we're not in a book now, are we? This is real life. This is you and me and we've got a job to do. This is where Luke Skywalker gets Chewie to join his gang.'

'What gang?'

Charlie takes Timothy's arm and leads him to the very edge of the wall and points to the open basement window.

'See that set-up, there?' says Charlie.

There are two minutes left before the Enviro 400 City Bus comes, so Timothy can afford to look at the set-up. The man points down to the front garden in the basement. There is a big window at the front of the house with no glass. Sticking out of the window, there is a chute made out of grey plastic a foot wide. The chute sits in a big blue bucket. The bucket is half full of soil, little stones and big rocks. A long wooden ladder splashed with paint leads from the front garden up to the pavement next to a massive yellow skip on the street.

Charlie keeps shaking his head like he doesn't want to believe that the set-up is true. He takes so long pointing everything out that there is only one minute before the bus is due, and Timothy is beginning not to listen. So while Charlie is still talking, Timothy goes to the corner of Gas Street and Yew Tree Lane. The bus that comes isn't the Enviro 400 City Bus. It's a Plaxton Paramount DAF 3500, which everyone knows isn't a rare bus at all. Timothy has been on so many Plaxtons he's lost count. So Timothy walks back to Charlie, who has his arms folded like he's Timothy's mother.

'Was that your bus?'

'No, it was a different one.'

'Listen, if you need a lift somewhere,' Charlie says, 'I can drop you there in my van later, but I could really do with a bit of help here, you know. I mean, do you realize what I've got to do? Look.'

Charlie points again at the set-up and explains it all to Timothy. 'I'm breaking up a solid concrete floor. Me, on my own. I'm shovelling it on to the chute. Chute to bucket, chute to bucket, chute to bucket, till the bucket's full. Climb out the friggin' window. Haul the bucket across the yard and climb up them bloody steps with it. And I tell you what, Flowers, mate, that bucket gets heavier when you go against gravity. At the top of the ladder, same problem. I've got to heft the bucket up on to this bloody shoulder here – the one with the bruises – and empty it into that skip there. Then I've got to just turn round and do the whole bloody thing again.

9

And again. Like I said, three hours. And I'm double your age. Double. You following?'

Timothy does follow.

'And if it rains, and it would be just my bloody luck if it did, I'll have the mud to contend with on top of everything else. It's the devil's own game, I tell you. So what I'm thinking is this.' Charlie puts his arm up and tries to lay it round Timothy's shoulder but his arm won't reach so he pats him on the back. 'If you could give me a few hours, we could break the back of this bloody job. I'd work with you, both of us together. I'd fill the bucket and you'd empty it. Twice as fast. I could let you have a few quid for your time. You win. I win.'

'Is it a race?' asks Timothy.

'A race? No,' says Charlie, 'it's not a race. It's a basement flat conversion. We're racing against the clock, Longfella, and that's the worst opponent there is. The clock never gives up.'

'But you said we'd both be winners,' says Timothy.

'Oh yeah, yeah,' says Charlie, nodding. 'Yeah, well, if we fill the skip by the end of the day and get that bloody concrete up, I win with my blood pressure returning to normal, and you win twenty quid. How's that?'

'Twenty quid,' repeats Timothy. He knows

what twenty pounds will buy, because one model bus is four pounds ninety-nine and he's good at maths. 'I have to tell my mum if strangers talk to me, or if anyone tries to get me to do things like last time.'

'Last time?'

'I got into trouble.'

Charlie points to the skip. 'Well, does that look like trouble?'

'No.'

'And do I look like a stranger to you, Longfella?'

Timothy can see the black of Charlie's eyes and the smudge of black under his nose that looks like a moustache. And he can see wrinkles around the man's eyes that Timothy's mum calls laughter lines.

'Not really,' says Timothy.

'Well, there you go! Look, you can tell your mam if you like. Of course you can, but if you do and she says you can't have your twenty quid, what then?'

'I won't be a winner.'

'Exactly.'

Timothy looks at the set-up again and the blue bucket of rocks. He doesn't know what his mother would say about him helping Charlie, but she did tell him to go for a long walk. She also knows he's saving up for some more model buses. And she always does the house from top to bottom on Friday mornings before she goes to work and he gets in her way. That is why he's standing at the corner of Gas Street and Yew Tree Lane in the first place.

'All right,' says Timothy, and Charlie rubs his hands together as if he's gone cold all of a sudden.

'Saved the bloody day you have, Timothy Flowers. Hero, you are. Right, fag first, Longfella, then we can start.'

Chapter Two

While Charlie lights a cigarette, Timothy goes back to the corner to see if there are any buses coming in case the Enviro 400 is late. But there's nothing coming. Probably he's missed it for today. Or it will be driving along another route so everyone can have a turn getting on and off at the back instead of the front, and playing on the internet while they're going to the shops. Maybe one day every bus will be an Enviro 400 City Bus with electric engines that are so quiet they can drive past you without you knowing about it.

Timothy hasn't always been interested in buses. He used to like dogs, but his mum became allergic after their dog died and he couldn't have another one. He still likes dogs, but sometimes dogs don't like him.

Last year, when they went on the caravan holiday, two big dogs started barking at him. When their owners came, they said it was Timothy's fault, but it wasn't. They were two men and they were much older than Timothy, with

13

shaved heads. One was wearing a blue tracksuit and the other one had black glasses. They said he had to go into the resort shop and steal a bottle of wine for them.

That's when Timothy got into trouble. Both dogs were the same, probably half German shepherd and half lurcher. Or half German shepherd and half Dobermann. Something like that. Timothy can remember the names of all the different dog breeds and all the different names of buses.

Charlie screws his foot over the last inch of his cigarette. 'Right,' he says, 'you better get that coat off because you'll be sweating like a peasant in ten minutes. And roll your sleeves up as well. We're working men, Flowers, my friend, working men.'

Then Charlie jumps back on to the ladder, drops into the basement yard and disappears through the window into the house. Timothy carefully climbs down after him, step after step, and folds his waterproof jacket into a neat square. He puts it behind the ladder where there is no rubble and no grass.

'Start with the bucket,' Charlie shouts from inside. So Timothy picks up the blue bucket and climbs back up the ladder, empties it into the yellow skip and climbs down again.

'Bucket back under the chute.'

Timothy does as he's told.

'Now in here.'

Timothy climbs through the window. Charlie is standing in the middle of the floor scooping up stones and bits of concrete and tossing them into the chute. The room is enormous, like Timothy's bedroom and his mum's bedroom rolled into one. Charlie's working like a toy robot when it's got new batteries, but there is a lot of floor and not very much of Charlie. When Charlie speaks, he sounds out of breath.

'This job . . . has got . . . to be . . . finished . . . by . . . four o'clock . . . latest.'

'Because then it will be dark,' says Timothy.

'Yeah,' says Charlie and stands up. 'That's one reason. So, come on then. Chop, chop. We've got to smash this floor into pieces. Use that there.' Charlie points at a massive hammer with a long handle leaning up against the wall. It feels good in Timothy's hand, like it was made for him.

'That's called the Brute, that is, Longfella. Feel the weight of him?'

'Yes.'

'Now,' says Charlie. 'You use him like this.' Charlie swings his arms in the air and bashes the invisible Brute on the ground. 'Bang!' he says. 'Bang! Bang! You're breaking up the concrete, Longfella. Bang! Bang! Like this.'

Timothy lifts the big hammer and smashes it down on the floor. All the concrete splits and cracks, little pieces fly in the air and Charlie jumps backwards.

'Sweet Jesus!' Charlie starts laughing and puts one hand over his chest. 'Bloody hell, Flowers! Bloody, bloody hell!'

Timothy smiles. 'Have I done it right?'

'Oh yes, oh yes, indeed. That's what I wanted. Go on, lad. You carry on, but let me just move out of the way a bit.'

Charlie stands in the corner of the room and nods at Timothy. *Mash! Bang! Crack! Smash!* It takes a little while for Timothy to find the right rhythm because when he raises the Brute it keeps hitting the ceiling. In the end, Timothy lets the handle slide through his hands on the downward swing, and then clunks it down on the concrete. *Smack! Smack! Smack!* Every three or four strikes, Timothy turns a little bit to the right. When he stops after about thirty blows he's standing in the centre of a destroyed circle of concrete. Timothy turns round and looks at Charlie in the corner. Charlie's made himself really small as if he's scared of something.

'I said stop!' he shouts. 'Didn't you hear me? You're breaking up the bloody concrete, boy!

Just the bloody concrete! Not the fucking foundations!'

Once Timothy's dad told him he was a fucking idiot. Timothy used to have a Saturday job at his dad's garage. One week Timothy made a scratch on one of the cars, but not on purpose. Usually when Timothy caused an accident his mum would say things like 'Nobody's fault' or 'Take your time'. But Timothy's dad started shouting and some spit came out of his mouth when he was shouting and it landed on Timothy's cheek. And then Timothy's dad pushed him and told him to stay out of his fucking way. Timothy started to cry and his dad started to laugh. When they went home, Timothy's dad was still angry. Timothy was only twelve and he still hasn't forgotten.

Timothy doesn't want to stay in the room with angry words, so he turns round and walks towards the open window.

'Wait!' shouts Charlie. 'Wait!' He runs across the room and holds on to Timothy's arm. 'Aye, where you going, Longfella? Don't go! Sorry, sorry for shouting. I didn't mean that. I was just a bit shocked at the power of you, like. You don't know your own strength, Timothy, mate. I mean, have you seen what you've done? Look.'

Timothy can see now that the room looks different. There is a big hole in the floor like on a film when someone's thrown a grenade in the Second World War.

'You're a machine!' says Charlie and he starts to laugh. It's a chuckle at first. 'A bloody great machine!' Then Charlie throws his head back and roars, splaying his fingers over his chest.

Timothy doesn't get jokes usually, but Charlie is slapping him on the back and pointing and for a whole minute Timothy laughs with him. They laugh together until Charlie's laugh turns into a cough and he lights a cigarette.

Afterwards, Charlie shows Timothy how to break the big bits of concrete into smaller bits that Charlie shovels on to the chute. Then Timothy goes back to breaking up the floor, but he doesn't use all his strength, just half. In between rock-breaking, Timothy goes out every so often and empties the bucket into the skip. Then he comes back and starts all over again. Charlie is still scooping up the stones, but now he's taken his shirt off and his chest is going up and down really fast because he's working so hard.

'Can I have a go?' says Timothy.

Charlie stops dead. 'Be my guest, Longfella. Be my guest.' He holds the spade out to Timothy.

But this part of the job is harder than it looks because sometimes Timothy digs down too deep, and Charlie says he doesn't want the Australians moving in. So Timothy has to learn how to skim and level, to swing the spade on to the chute and load the bucket. But the bucket gets full really quickly, and Timothy spends a lot of time climbing out of the window and tipping the bucket into the skip.

While Timothy is breaking the floor, Charlie sits in the corner of the room on a big piece of rock. 'Don't know how stone can feel soft, Longfella, but after the morning I've had, it does. It really does.'

He lights a cigarette and watches Timothy working. 'Bet you got bullied at school, didn't you?'

'Yes,' says Timothy.

'You don't hear a name like Flowers every day. What did they call you?'

Timothy doesn't want to say all the different names he got called. Some of them were about his size. Mountain Man. Yeti. Missing Link. Gorilla.

'Let me guess,' says Charlie. 'Daisy. No, Pansy. Petal. Weed. I'm right, aren't I?'

'No,' says Timothy.

'All right, all right. Okay then, what about

Rosie? Bluebell? In my day, it would have been something really inventive. Take my name now, Charlie. Of course, it was Charlie Chaplin at first, like you said yourself, but see this?' He points at his hair. 'Black hair? Most of the time they called me Adolf or Nazi, but the one that really stuck was the Final Solution. I was Final Solution for quite a few years, then they just called me Final. Then Whistle, you know, like "final whistle" in a football match. In the end, most of the time the lads would just whistle when they wanted me, like I was a dog or something. And I would answer to it like a right bloody fool.' Charlie laughs again and coughs.

'Go on,' he says, 'you tell me a story. It makes the time go quicker.'

Timothy is doing all the work now, the breaking and the scooping and the emptying the bucket. 'I don't know any stories,' he says and climbs out of the window. He gets his waterproof coat from the safe place in the front garden and gives it to Charlie. 'You can sit on my coat if you like,' he says.

Charlie nods. 'You're a good kid,' he says. He pushes the coat under his bum, leans back against the bare brick wall and lets out a big sigh. 'Nice.'

Charlie goes quiet then for such a long time

that Timothy thinks he has fallen asleep. He doesn't want to swing the Brute in case it wakes him up.

One eye opens. 'What?' says Charlie.

'Nothing.'

'You carry on and I'll tell you a story about the Brute.' Charlie lights a cigarette and blows the smoke into a ring like a magic trick. 'Saved my life, he did. Thought he would kill me, but he saved my life.'

Timothy watches the smoke ring dancing in the air, getting bigger and thinner until it disappears. 'Do another one,' he says.

Charlie blows five rings one after another. They float towards the light and vanish through the window.

'Right,' says Charlie, 'so I was about your age, twenty-one, twenty-two, something like that. I'm working fourteen floors up over on Aston Cross. Two big towers, Mayfield Tower and Piccadilly Tower. For the purposes of this story, Longfella, we'll call them Building A and Building B. Two big ugly twins, ripped apart, open to the weather, no windows, no doors, no heating. February it was, and when the wind blew through those towers it was as cold as the devil's hand. And that's fuck– bloody cold. Really cold.'

Charlie shivers. 'Anyway, we're doing a total

21

refit, central heating system, new walls, windows, floors, the lot. Building A and Building B are covered in scaffolding from head to toe, both sides and right up over the top, up to the roof. And we're on a time penalty. Know what a time penalty is?'

'Yes, like in football.'

'No, not like in football. This is a building site we're talking about. A time penalty is where we get fined if we piss about and finish late. I mean, mess about. But if we get our arses into gear, work hard, don't have no lunch and finish quick, we get paid better. Like me and you being winners today. Get it?'

Timothy nods and shovels dirt into the chute.

'So the gaffer says, "If you got to go from Building A to Building B, Health and Safety says you go across the floor, into the lift, down to ground level, out the building, across the yard, into the next building and up again in the lift." Well, there's at least twenty of us. We got our tools. We got transformers, bags of sand, concrete, the whole lot. "Or," says the gaffer, "you can step over here." He takes us to a hole in one of the walls and he shows us an identical hole in the other building. And between the buildings and the scaffolding there's a gap that ain't more than three feet across.'

Charlie takes a long suck on his cigarette and blows all the smoke out at once. 'The drop between them buildings makes your balls shrink, Flowers, mate.'

Timothy nearly got run over once, so he knows what Charlie means.

'The thing was, the gap was so narrow that by the end of the first day I got used to it and didn't look down. By the end of the first week, I'd stopped even thinking about it. I'd hop over just like that.' Charlie snaps his fingers. 'And after a bit, I forgot there was a gap. It felt like Building A and Building B were one and the same.'

Charlie shuffles in his seat and throws a stone straight on to the chute to save Timothy the trouble of scooping it up.

'So, it's Friday. Chop, chop, says me, it's half three and my throat's as dry as, well, as dry as your throat is about now. You thirsty?'

Timothy nods. He's been thirsty for about an hour.

'Me too. Anyway, where was I? Yeah, so, dry throat. Packing up time. I'm desperate to get to the pub. But before I can skedaddle, I've got to put my gear away. I hop over from A to B, pick up my tool belt, fasten it round my waist and grab the Brute. I turn round and step over the gap. Only the step I took going from A to B is not the same as the step back. Carrying my gear now, aren't I, and I haven't allowed for that. Didn't do my maths, did I, Longfella? Didn't put the right oomph into that step. I didn't allow for the Brute. For the weight of the Brute. He's going to kill me.'

Suddenly, Charlie's phone rings. He answers it and holds his finger up as if he's marking his place in the story. Timothy watches Charlie's face change. He swallows and stands up like he's in school and keeps trying to talk to whoever's on the phone.

'Yeah, it's coming on. Nearly finished.'

'No, no, it's all . . .'

'What?'

'Come off it, Brendan, I can't just –'

Then Charlie stops trying to talk and closes his eyes. The person on the phone is talking and talking, and after a long time, Charlie says, 'When?' He runs to the window and looks up. 'Now? You said four o'clock!'

He turns his phone off and quickly puts on his shirt. 'Shit! Shit!' he says. He puts his jacket on top and wipes his sleeve across his face. He stands in front of Timothy and says, 'My face?'

'It's dirty,' says Timothy.

'Well, fucking sort it out then!' Charlie closes his eyes and juts his face right up towards Timothy.

24

Timothy's seen what mothers do to their children, so he spits on the bottom bit of his shirt and wipes Charlie's face, especially the moustache under his nose. He pats Charlie's hair where the curls have tried to escape from their proper place. He brushes some of the wall dust off Charlie's shoulders.

'He's here. He's here,' Charlie whispers and then shouts really loud. 'Brendan, Brendan, come in!'

Chapter Three

The man who tries to climb in through the window is fat. He looks like a headmaster or a policeman's boss off the telly. He can't get his legs over the windowsill and Charlie has to help him.

The man walks in, looks around the room and then stares at Charlie. He doesn't say anything because he must have said it all on the phone. Charlie doesn't say anything either. Then the man looks Timothy up and down and says, 'Six six?'

Timothy raises his foot to show him which shoes he's wearing. But before he can speak, Charlie slaps Timothy's leg and says, 'Yeah, six six. Carry on, Tim, mate.'

So Timothy does as he's told but he can still listen.

'First week of November, you said, Charlie, and it's the third today,' says the man. 'You're a liar on top of everything else.'

'I'm not bloody lying, Brendan. You know this business. It will be ready. There's just a couple of windows, a few bits and pieces, and then this room and it's done.'

'Oh, really? Plastering? Finishing? How long will all that take?' The man is walking around the room, looking at the walls and the ceiling.

'I'll have this sold before Christmas and your share in your bank account the same day. I said I would, and I will, so don't –'

'Don't what?' says the man. 'Don't be surprised if you turn out to be the low life I always suspected you were?'

Charlie has his hands in his pockets and he's kicking stones around the room. Timothy has been told off so many times that he knows exactly what Charlie is thinking. First of all, he's thinking that the man should shut up. Secondly, he's thinking of what he can say to make the man shut up. Thirdly, he's thinking of something else that's nothing to do with the problem, like what he's going to eat for his dinner or that maybe they should both have a break and get some Coca-Cola. Fourthly, he's wondering how long the telling-off will last.

The man is still talking. He has the same accent as Charlie and he's old enough to be Charlie's father. Maybe he *is* Charlie's father because he's talking to Charlie like Timothy's father used to talk to Timothy. He's asking

27

questions that Charlie doesn't know the answer to and he's not even waiting for the answer anyway. Charlie keeps looking at his shoes. Eventually, the man shuts up.

Charlie shakes his head. 'I didn't want any of this to happen, Brendan, as God's my witness. But it has. And I'm trying to fix it. What more can I say?'

Timothy realizes the bucket is full and climbs out of the window. The man watches him and says to Charlie, 'How long have you had him? I haven't seen him before.'

'New lad,' says Charlie and follows Timothy through the window, helping the fat man out after him. They all climb the ladder with Timothy in the lead.

The fat man looks in the skip and then looks at Charlie. 'Where are the others?' He points at Timothy and says, 'He might be a bloody giant, but he's not a crew. How many of them turned up this morning? None, I imagine. You can't pay them, can you, Charlie?'

'They're on their lunch, Brendan. Just sent them. Me and the lad were just tidying up.'

'When's the concrete coming?'

'Tomorrow.'

The fat man looks at Charlie for a long time without blinking. 'She hasn't come out of her bedroom, you know. You say you're going to fix it, but you can't fix her, can you? And if you try to contact her, I'm going to break your ankles. Crush, actually. I'm going to crush your ankles, Charlie.'

'All right, Brendan. Crushed ankles. I get it.'

'And if I don't get your money by tonight, the same thing: crushed ankles. And by your money, I mean your half of the mortgage and all the back payments that I've made, like the mug you've taken me for. Understand that, Charlie? If you're so good at fixing things, fix that by tonight.'

Charlie doesn't say anything.

'Seven,' says the man. 'Seven o'clock. No later.'

Charlie shakes his head. All the time he's speaking he keeps shaking his head. 'Even though this will be done, finished, in the next four weeks? Even though the estate agent says he could sell it fifteen times over? He'll sell it in a bloody afternoon. How many jobs have I done for you? Nine? Have I ever come in late before? Don't act like I'm ripping you off, Brendan.'

'I've got one daughter, Charlie. That's the difference. Seven o'clock.'

The man walks across the road and gets into the back of a silver car that looks like a BMW 6 Series, and it drives away.

*

Timothy doesn't watch the car, he watches Charlie. Once, when Timothy was at the Round Oak Centre, there was a fire. Timothy was in the toilet when the alarm went off. Some people like to go to the toilet sitting down and not standing up, and Timothy's mum said it was up to each person to decide. The alarm made Timothy frightened. He was so scared, he couldn't get the toilet door open. He pulled it and pulled it, but he forgot to take the lock off and eventually the whole door came off in his hands. Timothy ran outside on to the lawn where everyone was waiting.

There wasn't really a fire. Someone had been smoking in the television room. It was probably Gary. When they found the toilet door had been ripped off its hinges and thrown against the mirrors, they asked who had done it. Everyone looked at Timothy until he said it was him. His mum had to come to the Round Oak Centre and sit with him while he got told off. Timothy knew that every time he went to the toilet in the future, he was going to be scared to bolt the door. But he also knew that, if he didn't bolt the door and someone came in, someone like Gary, he would get teased for sitting down.

So Timothy knows that Charlie is worried and scared. He looks like he's worried about three things. Getting the floor finished. Getting told off by Brendan. Meeting Brendan at seven o'clock with his money.

'What you looking at?' says Charlie. 'Get in the van.'

Charlie's van is white. The writing on the side says 'DIAMOND PROPERTY SERVICES' and there is a picture of a diamond underneath. Inside the van, there are lots of papers on the floor, newspapers and pink papers and white papers that say 'TO DPS, INVOICE OVERDUE' or 'REMINDER'. Charlie tells Timothy to pick them up and stuff them in the glove box.

'That's my favourite filing cabinet,' he says. 'Better known as the Bermuda Triangle. Things go in there but they never come out.'

There are some Extra Strong Mints in the glove compartment as well. Timothy can't stop thinking about them.

'Can I have them sweets?'

'Please.'

'Can I have them sweets, please, Charlie?'

'Yeah, go on.'

The cafe on Marsh Hill has steamed-up windows. The only cafe that Timothy usually goes to is in the precinct. He goes with his mum for a treat. She has coffee and walnut cake, and

Timothy has two doughnuts. Charlie opens the door and marches right up to the counter. He points at a table and tells Timothy to sit down.

There are two plastic sauce bottles, one red and one brown, salt and pepper and sugar and a plastic menu card. Timothy looks at the pictures. The breakfasts look very nice, but the dinners are the best because they all come with chips. If he had chips, probably no one would stop him from having lots and lots of red sauce, but Charlie hasn't asked him what he wants and Timothy doesn't want to shout because everyone will look. Timothy puts his hand up and waits for Charlie to turn round.

Two men on the next table start to laugh. They are wearing dusty clothes and check shirts. Then four men on another table start laughing as well and one shouts over, 'Do you need a piss, mate? It's out the back.' One by one, everyone looks at him and Timothy begins to feel like his arm is stuck in the air and won't come down.

'Oi,' shouts a man at the back of the cafe. 'Have you got the right answer? Go on then, tell us!'

Charlie turns round and walks back to the table with two big mugs of tea. He puts the tea on the table and grabs Timothy's arm and pushes it down. 'What you doing?'

'Can I have chips, please?'

'Drink your tea.'

Timothy pours the sugar into his tea until Charlie tells him to stop. 'No wonder you're a feckin' giant,' he says. Charlie hunches over his mug and takes a deep breath. 'Christ,' he says. 'I'm bloody starving. When did I last eat? What did I last eat?'

'I don't know,' says Timothy.

'I'll tell you what it wasn't. It wasn't steak and kidney pudding with buttery mash and gravy. It wasn't rhubarb crumble and custard. It wasn't roast pork with crackling and sage and onion stuffing neither. And it wasn't a sausage casserole with crusty bread. Nope. It was a meat and potato pasty in its plastic wrapper fresh from my brother's filthy microwave. That's what it was. Whatever else you can say about Shona Gleeson, she could cook the arse off any other woman I've ever known. It's a miracle I'm not thirty stone myself. You've seen her father.'

'Can I have chips, please?'

'When the love is gone, Longfella, the love is gone. I tried to tell her. But she was like "Oh, Charlie, why don't we get our own place?" and "Oh, Charlie, you don't mean it." In the end I had to do the dirty. Do the dirty and not hide what I'd done too carefully. Let her think she found out by mistake. Sometimes, it's the only way.'

Timothy is feeling really hungry now.

Charlie doesn't even drink his tea. He just turns the mug round and round on the table, staring at the bubbles on the surface.

'Makes you wonder if it's all worth it, you know, Longfella. All this aggro. Tired of it, I am. I shouldn't be taking my shirt off at my age, getting blisters on my bloody hands like a navvy. Maybe I should chuck it all in. Disappear. Somewhere I can get the bloody sun in my bones. Italy, Spain, somewhere like that. Yeah, Spain. Costa something. Start again on my own.'

The lady from behind the counter brings two big plates of dinner to the table. Neither has chips. Charlie picks up his knife and points at all the things on Timothy's plate. 'Faggots, mash and kale. That's right, kale in a place like this. Gravy. Eat it.'

Timothy likes the smell but he doesn't like the look of the faggots. He wonders what they would look like if they weren't covered in gravy. Probably they would look like two balls of dog food. Timothy watches Charlie cut one in half, load it with mashed potato and a bit of cabbage and then stuff the whole lot in his mouth. When

Charlie looks up, he stops chewing and speaks with his mouth full.

'Pork meat, pork liver, breadcrumbs. Good for you. Eat it.'

In the end, there aren't enough faggots. There isn't enough mash and there isn't enough gravy, but there is too much green cabbage. Timothy would like to leave it, but Charlie taps the side of Timothy's plate with his knife and lifts his eyebrows into a question so Timothy has to eat every bit. When they've both finished, Charlie calls for two more cups of tea. Then they have to stand outside the cafe with their mugs so Charlie can have a cigarette.

Charlie leans against the wall, but Timothy stands on the edge of the pavement in case the Enviro 400 City Bus comes past.

'Two more hours should do it,' says Charlie. 'Finish by five. Don't you want to ring your mum? Tell her where you are?'

'I haven't got a phone,' says Timothy.

'Here, use mine.'

But Timothy's mother isn't at home any more. She will have finished the house and she will be at work at the supermarket. She will be on the Customer Service Desk where everyone has to go if they have a problem, or if the beep goes off when they try to leave the shop. Not everyone is trying to steal a pair of jeans, Timothy's mother says. Sometimes there are genuine mistakes.

'I don't know the number,' says Timothy.

'Well, never mind, Longfella. I'll drop you back at the house and then I've got to see a man about a dog.'

'I had a dog once.'

'Not a real dog. The sort of dog that lends you money. The sort of dog that has very sharp teeth if you don't pay it back and it can snap, snap! Bite you on the backside. That sort of dog is called a bank manager, Flowers.'

Timothy watches as Charlie takes the mugs back to the counter. As he walks past the man who shouted at Timothy, he trips up and spills some of the cold tea on the man's neck. The man doesn't look very pleased, but Charlie just laughs and makes a rude sign.

Chapter Four

Charlie parks outside the house with the basement and tells Timothy to get out.

'I'll be back in a bit. You just carry on.'

Timothy doesn't move.

'What you waiting for? Same job as before. Go on.'

'I don't want to go down on my own.' Timothy is thinking of the broken room and the Brute hiding in the corner.

Charlie looks up at the ceiling of his van and shakes his head. 'Christ. Come on then. But I'm not paying you to be sitting on your arse all bloody day.' He starts the engine and drives off. 'When we get back, you'll have to work twice as hard and twice as quick. Got it?'

The NatWest Bank is all clean and bright. There is a lady at the door asking everyone what they want and asking them to sit and wait. After about ten minutes, Charlie goes into an office with a glass door and shakes hands with a man behind the desk. Timothy would like to go in to hear what they are saying, but Charlie told him to sit still and wait.

Timothy has a bank account of his own, but he never takes money out, he only puts money in. If he wants any money, his mum gives it to him. His mum says he's got hundreds of pounds and one day he might need it, if he was ever to live on his own. Even the thought of living on his own makes Timothy worried. Some people live at the Round Oak Centre, but Timothy prefers to live with his mum now that his dad doesn't live with them any more.

Lots of people come into the bank and go to a machine that says 'FREE CASH'. They press some buttons and take notes out of the machine. Timothy gets into the queue for the Free Cash. When it's his turn, he looks at the buttons and presses the number one and then two zeros. One hundred pounds. He can give that to Charlie to give to the fat man at seven o'clock. No money comes out, so he presses the buttons again. The screen just keeps saying 'WELCOME', so Timothy keeps pressing. When his mum goes to the bank she puts a card in first, but Timothy doesn't have a card. Eventually, the bank lady comes over and moves him away from the cash machine.

'Do you bank with us, sir?' she says. 'Are you on your own?'

'He's with me,' says Charlie, who has appeared from nowhere with the man from the desk. Charlie points at the chair. 'I told you to stay there.'

Timothy doesn't have time to explain about the Free Cash because Charlie is shaking hands with the man from the office. 'By the end of the day then?' Charlie says to the man.

'I'll see what I can do,' he answers.

Timothy can't hold it in any longer. 'Charlie! Charlie! If you put your card in the machine you can get free cash. Then you won't have to disappear to Spain.'

'Okay, okay,' says Charlie and tries to push Timothy towards the chairs.

'And that man won't crush your ankles at seven o'clock.'

The man from behind the desk is looking at Charlie and frowning. 'I didn't know you were going to Spain, Mr Pearson. When is this?'

'Ah, no, no. I'm going nowhere. I'm looking after this young lad for the day and, well, you can see how I'm fixed.' Charlie winks at the bank manager and nods his head towards Timothy. 'He tends to get the wrong end of the stick.'

The bank manager looks at Timothy. 'Yes, well.'

'So the end of the day, then?' asks Charlie. 'In my personal account?'

'I'll have to put a few checks in motion,' says the bank manager, going back to his office. He raises his hand and says goodbye. 'I'll be in touch.'

Charlie doesn't say anything until they are both sitting in the van at the traffic lights.

'You got a big mouth, Longfella, mate,' he says. His lips hardly move when he speaks and he doesn't even turn his head. 'Learn to do as you're told, and this day will be over a lot quicker for both of us.'

Charlie isn't the first person to tell Timothy to do as he's told. It's what Timothy's dad used to say all the time. Sometimes he would hit Timothy's mum in between each word. Do. *Hit*. As. *Hit*. You. *Hit*. Are. *Hit*. Told. Sometimes there would be a hit at the end and sometimes not, depending on how tired he was. Timothy's mum always used to say sorry, but it made no difference, and then it was Timothy's turn. When Timothy's dad was hitting him, she would always cry and shout, 'Not in the head, Graham. Not in the head.'

It's hard for Timothy to remember what people tell him to do. The Round Oak Centre is the place where he always seems to be able to remember instructions. He's been going there since he was fourteen when he came out of hospital. On Monday he goes for the afternoon because it's his turn on the computers. On Wednesday he goes all day for activities and Thursday morning he can go if he wants to, because he helps out with the new people or sometimes in the vegetable garden.

Every year there is a football match between the Round Oak Users and the Round Oak Staff. 'Users' means people who use the centre and 'Staff' means people who are in charge. But Gary thinks he's in charge. He tells all the users what position they have to be in, and Timothy always has to be in the goal because Gary says he blocks out the sunlight. This year Timothy let three goals get past him, and at half-time Gary called him names. He threw the football at Timothy's face and said, 'Hold on to it, you bloody orangutan! Hold on! Two hands, one ball! How hard can it be? Hold on and don't let go till I say. Idiot!' In the second half, Timothy did it right and Gary stopped shouting.

The only other days that are left to find something to do are Tuesdays and Fridays. Tuesday is the best day, because it's just him and his mum and no one else and he can choose what they do. It might be programmes on the telly, it might be a visit to a bus station, it might be going to the cafe for cake. In the summer, they always have a trip to see Auntie Janet and Timothy's cousins who are both married. Timothy would like to get married one day and his mum says that when he's older he might meet a nice girl at the Round Oak Centre.

Friday is the day when Timothy is on his own and his mum says he has to go out and see something of the world.

Charlie and Timothy park outside the basement house and go down the ladder again. Timothy empties the bucket and Charlie passes him the Brute.

'Off you go. He's all yours.'

Timothy decides to break up the floor the very best he can so Charlie isn't in a bad mood any more. He's gentle with the Brute. He doesn't go down too deep, and he scoops all the broken bits up really quietly. He is so quiet that he can hear everything that Charlie says. He's making lots of phone calls to his friends. Some of the phone calls are really quick and some of them take a long time.

'All right, Mick,' says Charlie. 'How you keeping? Me? Good, yeah. No, no, it's all going well. Nah, still on the basement conversion, just about to finish. Got the concrete pour tomorrow so, yeah, all good. Well, I say all good but to be honest I've got a bit of a cash-flow problem.

You know how it is, the bastards let you down, don't they? Yeah, you can say that again. Anyway, I was wondering if you could help me out? Couple of grand if you've got it. Fifteen then. Listen, mate, I'll take what you've got. Anything.'

All the time Charlie is talking, he's walking around in circles like he's a dog playing a game. And he's nodding even though the man on the other end of the phone can't see him. He stops suddenly.

'Mick, mate! Twelve hundred is grand. Better than grand. I owe you, mate, I owe you. You'll have it back before you do your Christmas shopping, mate. Guarantee it. Thanks, mate. I'll call in before you shut up shop. See you later.'

Then Charlie starts ringing another number and puts his thumb up to Timothy. 'Couple more of those and I'll be all right, Longfella. Wish me luck.'

But before Timothy can say anything, Charlie holds up his hand.

'Pete! You all right, mate? How's the kids? Good, good. Oh, you heard about that? No, sofa surfing till I get myself sorted. Nah, just one of them things, ran its course. Brendan? You know what he's like. He's taken it worse than she has. That's what I'm ringing you about. He's come over all Mafia. Yeah, chucking his weight around, all nineteen bloody stone of it. Listen Pete, the fact is that I need a bit of cash. Well, all in all I need seven grand by tonight. I've got about fifteen hundred so at this point, I'm not fussy, know what I mean.'

While Charlie is listening to the man on the phone, he makes the sign of the cross over his chest. Timothy stops because he's very worried for Charlie and it's very exciting.

'Three? You're kidding. Pete, mate, I love you. Seriously, you've lifted me out of the sticky brown stuff, you have. Yeah, I'll come to the bar tonight, sixish. Thanks, Pete. I mean it. Thanks.'

Charlie puts his phone in his pocket and places both of his hands together and closes his eyes. 'And thank you, God Al-bloody-mighty, wherever you are.'

Chapter Five

Timothy has emptied the bucket about five times and lots of the floor is now in the skip. Charlie lights a cigarette and sits down on his rock in the corner of the room.

'All comes down to relationships, Flowers, my friend. Me and Pete go back twenty years. I've done more jobs with Pete than you've had wet dreams. I mean, hot dinners. Remember that job I told you about, Building A and Building B and the Brute? That was me and Pete. We were apprentices together, but he had the bloody good sense to get out of this business and behind a nice warm bar on Corporation Street. He asked me to come in with him, but I'd just met this girl. And that girl's father is Big Brendan with the big ideas and the big threats. That's a relationship I wish I'd never started, I can tell you.'

Charlie blows three rings one after another. The three rings look like halos that angels have on top of their heads.

'What happened to Pete? Did he do his maths?' says Timothy.

'What?'

'Did Pete put the right oomph in?'

Charlie laughs for a long time. 'I suppose he did because he didn't drop fourteen floors down and kill himself. So, yeah, he must have done his maths because he didn't die.'

'Did you die?'

'You mean did I nearly die?'

'I nearly died once.'

'When?'

'I went to hospital for two years.'

'Two years?' Charlie is looking at Timothy like he doesn't believe him, so Timothy shows him the scar on his temple. It's white now but it used to be red. 'What happened?' says Charlie.

'Not one hospital. My dad had to go to prison after and I had to go to a different school.'

Charlie doesn't look at Timothy. He just looks at his cigarette and smokes it slowly. 'That's tough, Longfella. Very tough.'

Then Charlie's phone rings.

'Jez, thanks for ringing back. Listen, I need the address of Johnnie Stone. I know, I know, but I'm up against the wall here. He owes me a lot of bloody money and he knows it. Slippery fecker, he is. He was quick enough getting me to fit out that student house of his, wasn't he? I've had to claw fifty quid out of him bit by bit and I've had enough. Yeah, I'll watch myself, no worries. Yeah, okay, go on. Fourteen, Prospect Road. All right, yeah, I didn't hear it from you – yeah, I get it.'

Timothy can hardly see the floor any more. It's getting darker and darker outside and there's no light in the room. Charlie puts the torch on his phone for the very last bit of scooping and Timothy climbs out of the room. He empties the last heavy bucket into the big yellow skip. Charlie puts a big piece of wood across the window so no one can get in after they've gone.

On the pavement, Charlie keeps looking at his watch. 'You on a curfew?'

'What?' says Timothy. *Curfew* sounds like something from the army.

'What time you supposed to be home?'

'I don't like the dark.'

'So about now, then? Listen, come with me and I'll drop you back, all right? Where do you live?'

'Number seventy, Springfield Road. By the old people's home. When I see the old people's home, I turn the corner. It's right there.'

'Right,' says Charlie as he opens the door to his van. 'Make a couple of calls with me and I'll take you home after. Get in.'

The first place that they go is a drive-through coffee shop. This is the best thing in the world and somewhere Timothy has wanted to go for many, many years. Charlie speaks into a microphone and tells the lady what he wants and then he just looks at Timothy.

'Well? What you having?'

'Can I have some Coca-Cola and some chips?'

Charlie turns to the microphone. 'Coke and large fries, please.' Then he looks back at Timothy and says, 'And a Super Max Burger with cheese and bacon, twelve wings and a Triple Choc Muffin.'

Timothy starts to laugh because it's all of his dreams coming true at the same time. A drive-through. Chips. A burger. Chocolate. And Charlie.

'You like that, eh?' says Charlie and he slaps Timothy on his leg. 'Happy birthday, Longfella.'

They sit in the car park while Timothy eats his meal. Charlie has a cigarette with his coffee and leans back against the headrest.

'Christ, I'm tired.'

There's only one burger so Timothy has to make it last. There's red sauce in two square plastic tubs and the wings are covered in barbecue sauce. Timothy's mum gave him his birthday present the day before, because it was going to the cinema and it was the last day of the film. Afterwards, Timothy had a frozen pizza that he helped his mum to make, but a frozen pizza is not a Super Max Burger with bacon, cheese, wings and fries.

'This is the best birthday present I've ever had,' Timothy says.

'Yeah?' says Charlie. 'What else did you get?'

'A film and socks and a voucher from the Round Oak Centre and a cake. My auntie said she will give me my present when I go to see her. And my nan said she's going to take me shopping so I can choose myself.'

'And nothing from your dad.'

'Gary said that he got five hundred pounds when it was his birthday. Gary said he's going to learn to drive.'

'Yeah?'

'Gary always says things.'

'Like?'

'I have to do what he says. He pushes me.'

'You'll find a shite like Gary under every rock, Longfella. You know, like them crawling things that look like beetles. If you were my kid, I'd show you a few moves for the Garys of this world. A few of these.' Charlie jerks his elbow forward. 'And a few of these.' Charlie jabs the air with a quick punch.

All the fries have gone. Apart from the muffin, there's only one bite of burger left. Timothy eats it and puts all the rubbish in the brown paper bag. If he saves the muffin, he can eat it when he gets home after he's shown his mum what he got.

'I've got four brothers and every one of them has kids but me,' says Charlie. 'And I'm the eldest. Sick of being a bloody uncle, I am. It's all right, like, but, Christ. I know what you're thinking. "Charlie, you had your bloody chance with Shona." Desperate for kids that girl was. Should have stayed where I was. What the fuck is wrong with me? I broke her heart.'

Charlie finishes his coffee and throws the cup on to the back seat. Timothy reaches behind and picks it up and puts it in his brown bag. Then Timothy looks at the muffin that he's trying to save. He has one bite, then he eats it all.

'I don't know what went wrong, Longfella. It wasn't enough and it was too much, all at the same time.'

Charlie is quiet for a long, long time and Timothy thinks he's gone to sleep. Suddenly he sits up, rubs his face. 'Come on,' he says and starts the engine. 'Let's go.'

Chapter Six

Charlie parks outside a shop that sells phones and they walk in. There are people on computers at the back of the shop and a big glass counter at the front. When Charlie walks in, the man behind the counter makes a rude sign with his fingers. Charlie holds his hands up. 'No swearing in front of the kid, Mick.'

'Eh?'

'A new lad I'm breaking in. He's a bit, you know, funny about it.'

'Religious?'

'Something like that. You got it?'

Mick looks Timothy up and down twice. 'He could be useful in a fight, eh, Charlie?' He puts his hand under the counter and passes Charlie an envelope. 'It's all there.'

'Thanks, mate,' says Charlie and puts the envelope in his pocket. 'Six weeks and I'll be square. Eight tops.' Charlie shakes hands with the man, who makes the rude sign again as they open the door.

In the van, Charlie counts the money, looks at

his watch and starts the engine. 'Right, Saint Peter now.'

Charlie parks the van in an alley and bangs his fist on a big metal door. When it opens, a bald man spreads his arms wide and pulls Charlie into his chest. He's really, really black with two earrings in one ear and a tattoo on his neck.

'Come, come!' says the black man, and Timothy follows Charlie into the pub. It's very dark inside and has the same smell as the Rose & Cushion at the corner of his road. Except stronger.

'Pete, this is Longfella,' says Charlie. 'Longfella, meet Saint Peter.'

Pete isn't as tall as Timothy, but he is as wide and, when he shakes hands with Timothy, it's a nice, strong feeling.

'Wotcha,' says Pete. 'Big guy, eh?'

'Yes,' says Timothy.

Pete goes behind the bar and pours something into two small glasses.

'You still off the pop, Pete?' says Charlie.

'Nearly a year now, Charlie, mate. Best thing I ever did. Here.' He passes a glass to Charlie and a glass to Timothy. Charlie drinks his very quickly but when Timothy tries to copy him, he starts to cough. The drink tastes spikey and hot and it burns Timothy's tongue and gums.

Charlie takes the glass from Timothy and puts

it back on the counter. 'That's your birthday drink. Your first and your last.'

Pete laughs and pours another one for Charlie. Then he puts a plastic bag on the counter and taps it twice. 'It's all there. How far off are you?'

'Two. Two and a half.'

'Tricky,' says Pete.

Charlie swallows his second drink in one gulp and wipes his lips. 'I'm off to see Johnnie Stone now.'

'What?'

'Got his new address off a mate of mine. I'm off up there now.' He shoves his glass towards Pete. 'Put another in there.'

Pete takes the glass and puts it on the other side of the bar. 'No. You ain't going tanked up, Charlie, mate. That bastard's too unpredictable. You know what he's like. You're not going alone?'

Charlie nods towards Timothy, but Pete shakes his head. 'I don't think so.' Pete nods at Timothy. 'No offence, mate. Listen, I'll come myself.'

But Charlie slaps the counter. 'No way. No way. It'll be all right. You've done enough.'

Pete looks Timothy up and down. 'All right, I've got an idea. Hang on here a minute.'

Pete walks out of the bar and Charlie takes his

place. He pours some more of the terrible drink into his glass and drinks it quickly.

'Can I have some Coca-Cola, please?' says Timothy. 'And can I have ice in it?'

Charlie gives him a long glass full to the top and Timothy glugs it down in five seconds because it takes the nasty burning taste away. He doesn't want to be greedy, but he really wants another one. Charlie reads his mind like a magic trick. He just makes Timothy another Coca-Cola and puts some money on the side to pay for it. Timothy drinks the next one really quickly as well. Then he wants to go to the toilet. Charlie points to the corner of the room.

The toilets are very dark and it takes Timothy ages to find the light switch. Timothy feels a bit different. He feels like it's the right day to go to the toilet standing up. He unzips his trousers, finds his willy and points it at the urinal. It's the absolute best wee he's ever had. The longest, the strongest and the most exciting. Timothy begins to laugh and, because he's shaking, some of the wee goes on his trousers. After he's finished, he has to wipe the wee off with toilet paper. Then he washes his hands, turns off the light and goes back to the bar.

Charlie and Pete watch him. Timothy is still smiling.

'What's the joke?' says Charlie. 'And what's happened to your bleedin' trousers?'

Timothy laughs. 'I don't care.'

'Christ,' says Charlie.

Pete is holding a leather jacket out. 'Here, try this on.' Timothy puts his arms into the jacket and it just fits. Timothy has always, always, always wanted a leather jacket, but his mum said they were too expensive. This might be another birthday present.

'Zip it up,' says Pete, but when Timothy has zipped it, Charlie and Pete both say, 'Halfway,' and Timothy has to pull the zip back down. Then Pete gives Charlie a tube of something and says, 'I got this off the missus. You do it.'

Charlie makes Timothy sit down on one of the chairs. He puts some gel in his hands and then wipes it all over Timothy's hair. Then he pulls it all back and puts even more gel on. He stands back and looks at Timothy. Then he looks at Pete. 'It's the eyes, Pete.'

'I know. You can't do anything about the eyes. He still looks better. I could put him on the doors looking like that.'

Timothy's head feels cold and wet. He walks to the toilets and when he looks in the mirror he wants to laugh again. Once, he saw half a gangster film with his cousins with lots of swearing and guns. His auntie told the cousins off for letting him watch it, but they didn't even say sorry. Timothy looks like a gangster now, with Pete's leather jacket and his hair wet and pushed back off his face. He makes his eyes go really small until he can hardly see. He knows what Pete and Charlie can see in his eyes.

Charlie kicks the door open. 'Come on, lover boy, get yourself out of the mirror. Time to go.'

When they're back in the van, Charlie turns round in his seat and lights a cigarette. He's facing Timothy and the whole van is filled with smoke.

'Now, listen, from now on you're an observer, right? What does *observer* mean?'

Timothy says nothing. Charlie points with his cigarette hand.

'It means you can watch. You can look. You stand next to me like the Queen's bloody soldier on parade. What does the Queen's soldier do? Nothing, that's what. Not a bloody thing. Some arsehole comes up with a camera and steps on his toe? Nothing. Dog pisses on his trouser leg? Nothing. Some twit flicks a chip in his face? Nothing. See no evil, hear no evil, speak no evil, all rolled into one. That, Longfella, is you. The bloke we're going to see is ugly in every way. Up here –' Charlie points to his face – 'in here –'

Charlie points to his head – 'and in here –'
Charlie points to his heart. 'He could be tame,
he could be wild. No way of knowing. All right?
So do as you're told. All right?'

'Yes.'

'You're not coming as my back-up. You're
coming as my mate, right, my silent, can't-speak,
can't-talk mate. Literally. You can't talk. Just
stand behind me, like this.'

Charlie folds his arms over his chest and puts
his head on one side. 'No more. No less.'

Timothy folds his arms to show him he under-
stands.

They drive under a flyover and along the dual
carriageway. All the lights have come on and
there's lots of traffic. Charlie drives like he's on
a computer game, weaving in and out of the
traffic and making people blow their horns.
Charlie shouts at them through the window or
makes rude signs with his finger. Eventually,
they come to a row of houses overlooking a
park. Charlie drives slowly, counting numbers
until he gets to number fourteen. 'Gotcha,' he
says. Charlie leans behind his seat and picks up
a big iron tool with a red wooden handle. He
slips it up his sleeve and pulls down his shirt.

Charlie rings the bell and says to Timothy,
'Who are you?'

'The Queen's soldier,' says Timothy.

The man that opens the door of number fourteen is wearing a white vest with white jeans and a big leather belt with a massive, massive buckle. The skin on his face has lots of little holes in it, and his eyes are red and very small. He's eating a bar of chocolate that looks like it's melting through his fingers. It's not a Mars Bar because it's too long, unless it's a Maxi Mars Bar or a Maxi Snickers. Snickers have got peanuts in and Timothy doesn't like nuts. Timothy keeps staring at the man because he has no eyebrows and he has no hair. His head looks like an old football that's been kicked around too much.

'All right, Johnnie,' says Charlie. Charlie's voice sounds different, deeper and harder.

The man leans forward until he is very close to Charlie and then says, 'What?'

Charlie puts his hands in his pockets. 'You know what. My invoice, Johnnie. We never squared up. There's some still outstanding.'

The man stares at Charlie for a long time and then looks up at Timothy. Then he looks back at Charlie. Then he looks back at Timothy.

'Who's the gorilla?' He stuffs all of the chocolate in his mouth at the same time even though it can hardly fit. He wipes the chocolate from his hands on his white jeans and vest. He stands with his feet apart and his hands hanging by his side. 'This your new boyfriend, Charlie? I heard you'd moved out of Brendan's and dumped that porky daughter of his.'

'Two thousand eight hundred quid, Johnnie,' says Charlie with his new voice. 'It's no joke now. It's been, like, six months.'

'I know how long it's been.'

'I need it now. Tonight.' The way Charlie moves his arm makes Johnnie Stone jerk back.

'You gonna start with me, Charlie boy?'

The two men look at each other like they're about to start a race. Timothy can see all the little scars on Johnnie Stone's face and his chest moving up and down in his vest.

'You're ugly,' says Timothy. 'Charlie said you're ugly in every way. And he's right.'

'That right?' says Johnnie Stone and he lunges forward and makes his head bang into Charlie's face. Charlie flies backwards and hits Timothy in the chest. Johnnie Stone moves forward and Timothy can see he is going to do it again. He's going to hit Charlie in his head and everyone knows how bad that is.

Timothy's hands come up all on their own and grab the man's head and he holds on to it tight, like he's in goal and he's going to stop Johnnie Stone from scoring. Both of Timothy's hands are on the man's head, one on his face and one on his scalp. Timothy knows that if he lets go the man will try and hurt Charlie. So he holds the man's head tighter and tighter, digging his fingers in until the man's knees bend and Timothy has to bend over too because he's nearly on the ground. Johnnie Stone is like Gary from the Round Oak Centre and he's like the men with the dogs that got him into trouble. Timothy could turn the ball of the man's head round and round and it might screw off like the top of a bottle of pop. Then Timothy could kick it across the street and into the park.

Charlie shouts really loud, 'STOP!' and Timothy takes his hands off Johnnie Stone's head. Johnnie falls backwards into the hallway of his house, holding his face and moaning, turning from side to side. Charlie's face is covered in blood. Some of it has splashed on to his very white shirt. He shoves Johnnie Stone into the house, and then Timothy and Charlie go inside. 'Get up! Get up!' says Charlie, closing the door.

Johnnie Stone has a massive, massive television and on the screen there is a naked lady. Someone has pressed 'pause' so she's not moving. On his glass coffee table there are broken cigarettes and full ashtrays and empty bottles of beer and a pipe. Everything is a mess and the room is so hot that Timothy wants to take off Pete's leather jacket.

Charlie shoves Johnnie Stone down on to his white leather sofa. Johnnie Stone has blood coming out of one eye. With the other eye he looks at Timothy and says, 'You're a bastard.'

'No,' says Timothy, 'I'm a soldier,' and that makes Johnnie Stone look at him differently, like he's the one who's scared, like he's the one who's the gorilla. Timothy looks at the naked lady and the chocolate on Johnnie Stone's white trousers that looks like he's pooed himself and he starts to laugh.

'I'm a soldier,' he says again to Johnnie Stone. 'I'm the Queen's soldier.'

All the time, Charlie is looking around the room and putting his hand under the sofa cushions. 'Where is it, Johnnie?' he says. 'And don't mess me about.'

Johnnie Stone points to a leather coat lying over a chair. 'There, in there. Take it and piss off.'

The lady's chest is very big, much too big for the television screen because it's pressed up against the glass and all blurred. Timothy can't see the detail of the woman or what she looks like. She must be very pretty.

Charlie counts some notes out of Johnnie

Stone's pockets. 'There's only eighteen hundred here, mate,' he says.

Johnnie Stone is sitting up, rubbing his head. 'Didn't know I was getting a visit from a fucking psychopath, did I?'

'I'll be back,' says Charlie, and Timothy has to stop looking at the lady on the television and get back into the van.

Charlie drives off really quickly and as soon as they get round the corner he parks the van. Then he takes the iron bar out of his sleeve and drops it on the seat behind him.

'Jesus Christ!' he says. 'Look at my bloody face! I told you not to say anything!'

'Sorry,' says Timothy.

But Charlie is laughing. 'You nearly killed Johnnie Stone!' He slaps Timothy on his leg five times. 'Bloody hell! Dangerous, you are. Right, let's count up.' He takes lots and lots of money out of different pockets and puts it all on his lap.

'Who was that lady?' says Timothy.

'Four thirty, four forty, four fifty –'

'She had no clothes on.'

'That's right. Six eighty, seven.'

'He was watching her with no clothes on.'

'Eighteen fifty –'

'She had very big –'

'Will you give it a rest! I'm trying to count

here! Yes, she was a lady with big knockers and he was watching her. It's called entertainment, Longfella, my friend. Adult entertainment. Naughty films for men like Johnnie Stone that show ladies being naked. Bloody hell. Now button it.'

Charlie carries on counting his money and then he counts it again. 'Five thousand nine hundred. It'll have to do. Come on.'

Chapter Seven

Ten minutes later, they stop the van outside a big house. Charlie gets out and presses a buzzer. Two big iron gates swing open and they drive in. They park next to three other cars and Charlie takes a deep breath. 'You can wait here, Longfella. This won't take long.'

'I don't like the dark, Charlie,' says Timothy.

'Come on, then. But please, if you do only one thing for me for the rest of your life, don't speak, keep it zipped.'

Brendan opens the front door. He is wearing an apron that is tied across his big belly. He stares at Charlie's bloody face and shakes his head. 'It isn't just me and my daughter that you're messing about, then, Charlie. Eh? Look at the state of yourself.'

He moves aside to let Charlie and Timothy come in. The house is really big with stairs that curve round. Even the hallway has a sofa in it. Maybe people have to sit there when they come to visit. Brendan walks into the kitchen and

Timothy follows. Timothy would like to count all the kitchen cupboards so he can tell his mum how many there are. But he can't count without saying the numbers out loud, so he just looks at them – the ones on the wall and the ones on the floor and the ones in a big square in the middle of the room. There is a big bunch of flowers in a vase. There's an enormous silver fridge and a cooker as big as the one at the Round Oak Centre that cooks enough for forty-two people.

Brendan stands in front of the stove and stirs something in a very big iron pot. It smells like the best dinner Timothy could ever imagine. Brendan looks at Timothy and says, 'Do you cook?'

'No,' says Timothy.

'You should learn. All men should know seven meals. That's what my mother said and she was right. All men should learn to look after themselves. How old are you?'

'I'm twenty-one. It's my birthday today.'

'Ah,' says Brendan. 'Twenty-one. Twenty-one.'

Brendan turns round and says, 'So, Charlie . . .'

But Charlie hasn't come into the kitchen. Through the doorway, Timothy can see Charlie staring up the staircase in the hallway. Timothy goes to see what he's looking at and a lady is standing halfway up the stairs. She's holding on to the bannister.

'Hello, Charlie,' she says.

Charlie doesn't say anything, but his face is saying that he likes her. Brendan rushes out from the kitchen. 'Shona! Upstairs. Didn't I say? Go on. Back up.'

'Hello, Charlie,' she says again.

Charlie nods. 'You look great, Shone. Really great.'

Shona has long brown hair and very big eyes. She points at the blood on Charlie's shirt and frowns. 'You're hurt, Charlie.'

Charlie doesn't move. He just keeps looking up at Shona. 'It's nothing,' he says.

'Shona!' shouts Brendan, but Shona holds her hand up.

'It's all right, Dad.'

Brendan shakes his head and says, 'Sweet Mother of God,' and walks back into the kitchen. As he goes past Timothy, he pulls his arm. 'Come and have some dinner. We could be a while here. Osso buco. Ever had it? No? Come on.'

Timothy sits at a long wooden table opposite Brendan. They both have big bowls of meat and gravy and rice and a glass of wine. Timothy would like some of the Coca-Cola that he saw in the fridge but he's too scared to ask. Brendan might lose his temper and try to crush Timothy's ankles. The meat has got big bones in it.

'Calf meat,' says Brendan. 'Some people think it's cruel. Taste it and judge for yourself. Go on. Tuck in.'

Timothy watches Brendan so he knows what to do. Brendan puts a napkin in his shirt collar and doesn't use his knife. He just uses his fork to put the food in his mouth and then picks up a bone and starts to suck it. Timothy does the same. It's very nice, like the stew that his auntie makes but better and tastier.

'How long have you been working with Charlie?' says Brendan with his wine glass in his hand.

Timothy closes his eyes so he can remember. 'Seven hours,' he says.

'Ah,' says Brendan. 'How many other blokes were you working with today?'

'Charlie says I'm like ten men.'

Brendan sips his wine and nods to Timothy's glass. 'Burgundy,' he says. 'Try it.'

Timothy takes a sip and then immediately has a bit more meat. It's not like the drink that Pete gave him, it's watery and bitter. It makes Timothy's mouth crumple up so he puts the glass down.

Suddenly Timothy hears Charlie laugh and

then Shona laughs as well. Timothy looks at Brendan, who shakes his head.

'Give me strength,' he says and then takes Timothy's plate. 'More?' he says.

He puts lots more of the meat stew on Timothy's plate and then pours Timothy a big glass of Coca-Cola and puts ice in it. 'You'd rather have this, I bet. There you go.'

Timothy drinks it all in one go.

Brendan finishes his dinner and takes his apron off. He lays it on the table and fills his glass with more wine. 'What's your story, lad? Where are you from?'

'I live with my mum,' says Timothy. 'Seventy, Springfield Road.'

'How do you know Charlie?'

'I was waiting for the Enviro 400 City Bus. It's electric, but it didn't come.'

'And he offered you a job?'

'He was trying to do it all himself, just him and the Brute. And the set-up was the devil's own game. But then he stopped work because he wanted to get the money so you don't crush his ankles. And then Pete gave me this jacket and Johnnie Stone hit him in the head.'

'Johnnie Stone, eh? That wasn't very nice.'

'Yes, and Pete gave Charlie some money and

the man in the phone shop. Charlie said he might go to Spain on his own. Charlie said Shona could cook the arse off any woman he's ever known.'

Brendan smiles. 'He's right about that.'

Timothy finishes his second dinner. 'And Charlie said that he broke her heart.'

'He's right about that as well. What else has Charlie been saying?'

'He said I was the Queen's soldier. And he said I had hidden talents. And he said, if I was his kid, he would show me some moves. And because it's my birthday he took me for a drive-through burger with fries. And wings. And a muffin. And he said I was bloody dangerous. And he said I was a working man. And a winner. Charlie said I'm a winner.'

Brendan stands up and, as he takes Timothy's glass, he puts his hand on his shoulder. 'You are, lad.'

First Shona comes into the kitchen and then Charlie. Everyone watches as Charlie counts all the money out on to the table in front of Brendan.

'I'm short,' says Charlie. 'You'll have to give me a few days. I did my best as God's my witness.'

Brendan doesn't look at Charlie or the money, he only looks at Shona, and Shona only looks at Charlie.

'Concrete tomorrow. Isn't that what you said?' says Brendan. 'How are you paying for that?'

'I'm waiting on a bank loan. Sorted it out today.'

Brendan pushes the money across the table to Charlie. 'I want it all square at the end of the job. Plus ten per cent.'

Charlie lets out a big breath. 'You sure, Brendan? I mean, we're on target, like, and the estate agent said –'

Brendan holds his hand up. 'I know, I know. Don't give me the bloody speech again, for pity's sake. Go on, clear off. Shona's tired, aren't you? And she's not eaten.'

Charlie looks at Shona and nods. 'Yeah, yeah, sure. I've got to take the lad home anyway.'

Brendan puts himself between Shona and Charlie. He puts his hand on Charlie's chest and points to the front door. 'Yeah, he's a good lad. You've got him to thank for my good mood.'

When they are back in the van and Charlie has stopped waving to Shona, Timothy takes off Pete's leather jacket. Since he's eaten Brendan's dinner, it feels too tight. He puts his own jacket on and zips it up to the neck.

'What did you say to him?' says Charlie.

'Nothing.'

'Did you see her? She said she's lost two stone. Didn't need to, but she looks better for it.' Charlie runs his fingers through his hair. 'She always could make me laugh.'

Chapter Eight

Charlie takes a funny way to Springfield Road. He goes over the flyover and along the dual carriageway and through the small roads of the big housing estate. He points at two big tower blocks and stops the van. 'Mayfield Tower and Piccadilly Tower. Remember? Look.'

The two blocks of flats are all lit up, and they are so close together that Timothy can hardly see a gap between them.

'That's where you nearly died.'

'It is.'

'What happened?'

'You're sure you want to know? You won't be scared now?'

Timothy shakes his head. He won't be scared.

'Well, like I said, I've gone over the gap from A to B, picked up my gear, turned round and stepped back over. Only the step I took going from A to B ain't the same as the step back. I'm heavier, aren't I? I'm loaded up. Weighed down. I forgot about my gear. Forgot about the Brute. Miscalculated, haven't I? So when I step over the gap, it's only my toes that catch the step. Just the toes. I can feel the Brute pulling me down. I'm going to fall. I'm going to die. My head and belly and my manhood and all the kids I've never had are going to smash into a thousand pieces on the concrete, fourteen floors below. I'm going to die, Longfella.'

Timothy can feel his heart hammering in his chest. Charlie lights a cigarette and points at his forehead. 'Ha! The thing that kills you is the same thing that saves your life, Flowers, mate.'

'Did you fall?' asks Timothy, although he can hardly breathe.

Charlie smiles. 'No, Longfella. I didn't fall.'

Charlie slams his hands on the steering wheel. 'I threw that bloody Brute! I threw him and I held on and the weight of the Brute pulled me forward. He saved my life. He pulled me over the line and on to the floor of the building. I landed with my arms round the Brute and my balls intact, my friend. My balls intact.'

Timothy looks at Charlie's face and from Charlie's face to Charlie's balls.

'Close your mouth, mate.'

Because they went the long way to Springfield Road, Timothy knows they will go past the garage. Not the bus garage where the Enviro 400

City Bus is and the Plaxton Paramount DAF 3500. They will go past Flowers Auto Centre, the garage that Timothy's dad owns where they sell cars and vans.

When his dad went to prison, the garage closed down. Then when he came out of prison, it opened again. Timothy knows this because his mum told him. Timothy was in hospital for most of the time that his dad was in prison, so he couldn't have gone to the garage if he'd wanted to. And he didn't want to. He doesn't want to now. Timothy's leg is jogging up and down on its own and his hands are all hot and sweaty. He wipes them on his trousers. Charlie looks down and sees.

'What?'

Timothy looks out of the window. 'We can go down Rochester Avenue. If we go down Rochester Avenue, we can still get there.'

'What's wrong?' Charlie is looking right and left. 'What is it?'

Any minute now Charlie will turn the corner and Timothy will see his dad's garage. Any minute now his dad might be in there. Charlie does turn the corner and stops at the traffic lights, and Timothy sees his dad sitting in the office with the light on. Timothy's dad is always at work, which is why he is so tired when he comes home. He lives with someone else now. He will be shouting at them about how hard he works, and about them not doing as they are told, and how they are making him angry all the time.

Timothy stares at his dad and Charlie looks at the garage too. 'Flowers Auto Centre,' says Charlie. 'Flowers. Who's that in there?'

Timothy looks away.

'Your dad?'

Timothy nods.

Then the car behind starts pressing its horn and Charlie has to drive off. But he doesn't drive very far. He parks the van down the road from the garage. Then he reaches behind his seat and gets the same tool that he took to see Johnnie Stone.

'Wait here,' he says, 'and I mean it this time. Wait here.'

Timothy is still afraid of the dark, but he's more afraid of seeing his dad and he knows that's where Charlie is going. Timothy watches Charlie walk into the office. He sees his dad stand up and he sees Charlie point with one finger right in Timothy's dad's face. Charlie is doing all the talking and Timothy's dad is walking backwards. Then a bus comes and Timothy can't see any more. It isn't the Enviro 400 City Bus. It's just a normal bus and it stays at the bus stop for ages, letting people get on and off.

Timothy has to wait. And for all the minutes that Timothy waits he has to try very hard not to cry. Charlie is clever and knows more than Timothy, except for one thing. Charlie doesn't know what Timothy's dad is like when he gets angry.

Timothy can't really remember much about when he went to his old school, when he was eleven, when his friends used to call for him, when his mum used to call him 'cheeky' all the time. Then one day, when he was twelve, everything changed. Timothy scratched the car and later he got hit in the head. He does remember that. He doesn't remember the first hospital, but he does remember the second hospital where he had to have lots of X-rays and medicine. Timothy kept having fits, but the doctor said they would stop and they did. Then he went to a different school and, when he left school, he went to the Round Oak Centre.

When Timothy came home from the hospital, he was nearly fourteen. Timothy and his mum had a social worker who always wore white trainers with Velcro fasteners. She was really nice. And there was another lady who used to come to the house and help Timothy get dressed, but he got so good at it that she stopped coming. She had a photograph of a Yorkshire terrier in her purse and she kept talking about Timothy's brain. She said it was different now and he would have to learn to do things again. She was nice and kept saying how she couldn't believe the progress he was making. Then one day she stopped coming and it was just Timothy and his mum.

Sometimes, when Timothy is washing up side by side with his mum, she grabs hold of him and hugs him. She thinks she hugs him too tight, but she doesn't. She says things like 'I'll never forgive myself but maybe you will one day'. Or she says 'You don't know how sorry I am, Tim'. But Timothy doesn't know what she's talking about, because everything is fine and he's happy.

After four minutes Charlie gets back into the van. He throws the tool on to the back seat and starts the engine.

'So!' he says. 'Have you had a good birthday, Longfella?'

'Why were you shouting?' says Timothy. 'You looked like you were shouting.'

'Who? Me? Nah, I went to see if I could drop the van off in the morning for a repair. That's all.'

They drive all the way to Timothy's house and, when they park outside, Charlie reaches into his pocket.

'Oh yeah, I forgot to give you this.' Charlie takes some money out. 'This is from your dad. He said "happy birthday". Told me to tell you.'

Timothy takes the money and holds it up to the light.

Charlie punches him on his arm but not very hard. 'One hundred quid that is, Longfella. One hundred quid. From your dad.'

'Thank you, Charlie,' says Timothy.

'And this is from me,' says Charlie, and he stuffs some more money in Timothy's pocket. Timothy can't see how much it is but, when he gets home, he will count it out slowly on his own in his room.

'Thank you, Charlie.'

Suddenly the door to Timothy's house opens and Timothy's mum comes out. She stares at the van and shouts, 'Is that you, Timothy? Timothy! Is that you in there?'

Timothy gets out of the van and walks up the garden path. His mum walks straight past him and up to Charlie. 'Who are you?' she shouts. 'What have you been doing with my son?'

Charlie gets out of the van and smiles. He puts his hand out so Timothy's mum can shake it. 'Charlie Pearson, missus. Diamond Renovations.' He points to the sign on the side of the van. 'Just dropping him off after a day's work.'

'Work?' says Timothy's mum. 'Work doing what?' She turns to Timothy and says, 'Where have you been all day? I've rung Round Oak ten times. Can you remember where you've been, Timothy?'

Charlie points behind him. 'Corner of Gas Street and Yew Tree Lane, Mrs Flowers. Basement conversion. Taking up concrete. Worked like a Trojan, he has. Saved my life.'

Timothy is nodding. 'I saw a naked lady.'

Timothy's mum is just about to speak when Charlie holds his hands up. 'It was on a television in a shop, missus. Just as we were walking past on our way to the cafe. I couldn't help it. Won't happen again.'

'Again?' says Timothy's mum.

Charlie gets back into his van. 'Eight o'clock tomorrow, Longfella,' he says. 'Don't be late. You know where. We're working men, my friend. Working men.'

Timothy watches Charlie's van drive away until the red lights at the back get smaller and smaller and disappear.

Timothy's mum asks him all about his day, and Timothy tells her about his dinner in the cafe and the faggots and mashed potato. He tells her that Charlie was nice to him and that he went to the drive-through in Charlie's white van. But he doesn't tell her about the swearing, and he doesn't tell her about the drink he had in the pub with Pete or about Johnnie Stone's football head.

Timothy's mum makes him have a shower, because he smells of cigarettes and because he has gel in his hair. She says it suits him and she will buy him some from the shop if he wants. She lets him stay up until *News at Ten*. When he's in bed, Timothy counts his money three times and puts it on his chest of drawers. He's going to learn to drive and save up for his own van.

Timothy gets into bed and turns off the light. When he closes his eyes, he imagines all the roads Charlie is driving along. Charlie will weave in and out of the traffic and swear at the other drivers. He will overtake all the buses, even the Enviro 400 City Bus. And he will overtake all the other cars and laugh when they don't like it.

About Quick Reads

Quick Reads are brilliant short new books written by bestselling writers. They are perfect for regular readers wanting a fast and satisfying read, but they are also ideal for adults who are discovering reading for pleasure for the first time.

Since Quick Reads was founded in 2006, over 4.5 million copies of more than a hundred titles have been sold or distributed. Quick Reads are available in paperback, in ebook and from your local library.

To find out more about Quick Reads titles, visit

www.readingagency.org.uk/quickreads

Quick Reads is part of The Reading Agency, the leading charity inspiring people of all ages and all backgrounds to read for pleasure and empowerment. Working with our partners, our aim is to make reading accessible to everyone. The Reading Agency is funded by the Arts Council.

www.readingagency.org.uk Tweet us @readingagency

The Reading Agency Ltd · Registered number: 3904882 (England & Wales) Registered charity number: 1085443 (England & Wales) Registered Office: Free Word Centre, 60 Farringdon Road, London, EC1R 3GA The Reading Agency is supported using public funding by Arts Council England.

We would like to thank all our funders and a range of private donors who believe in the value of our work.

LOTTERY FUNDED

THE
READING
AGENCY

has something for everyone

Stories to make you laugh

Stories to make you feel good

Stories to take you to another place

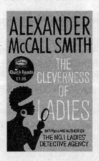

Stories about real life

ANDY McNAB
AUTHOR OF *BRAVO TWO ZERO*
TODAY everything changes

Street Cat Bob
HOW ONE MAN AND A CAT SAVED EACH OTHER'S LIVES. A TRUE STORY
JAMES BOWEN

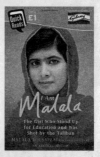

I am **Malala**
The Girl Who Stood Up for Education and Was Shot by the Taliban
MALALA YOUSAFZAI

Stories to take you to another time

OUT OF THE DARK
ADÈLE GERAS

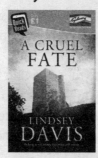

A CRUEL FATE
LINDSEY DAVIS

A DREADFUL MURDER
THE MYSTERIOUS DEATH OF CAROLINE LUARD
MINETTE WALTERS
THE NUMBER ONE BESTSELLING AUTHOR

Stories to make you turn the pages

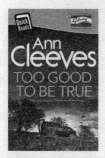

Ann Cleeves
TOO GOOD TO BE TRUE

DEAD SIMPLE
EIGHT KILLER READS FROM EIGHT BESTSELLING AUTHORS
EDITED BY HARRY BINGHAM

Amanda Craig
THE **OTHER SIDE OF YOU**

ONE FALSE MOVE
DREDA SAY MITCHELL

For a complete list of titles visit
www.readingagency.org.uk/quickreads

Available in paperback, ebook and from your local library

Why not start a reading group?

If you have enjoyed this book, why not share your next Quick Read with friends, colleagues, or neighbours?

The Reading Agency also runs **Reading Groups for Everyone** which helps you discover and share new books. Find a reading group near you, or register a group you already belong to and get free books and offers from publishers at **readinggroups.org**

There is a free toolkit with lots of ideas to help you run a Quick Reads reading group at **www.readingagency.org.uk/quickreads**

Share your experiences of your group on Twitter

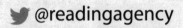 @readingagency

Continuing your reading journey

As well as Quick Reads, The Reading Agency runs lots of programmes to help keep you and your family reading.

Reading Ahead invites you to pick six reads and record your reading in a diary to get a certificate **readingahead.org.uk**

World Book Night is an annual celebration of reading and books on 23 April **worldbooknight.org**

Chatterbooks children's reading groups and the **Summer Reading Challenge** inspire children to read more and share the books they love **readingagency.org.uk/children**

KIT DE WAAL

MY NAME IS LEON

It's 1981, a year of riots and royal weddings. *The Dukes of Hazzard* is on TV. Curly Wurlys are in the shops. And trying to find a place in it all is nine-year-old Leon. He and his little brother Jake have gone to live with Maureen. They've lost one home, but have they found another?

Maureen feeds and looks after them. She has wild red hair and mutters swearwords under her breath when she thinks they can't hear. She claims everything will be okay. But will they ever see their mother again? Who are the couple who secretly visit Jake? Between the street violence and the street parties, Leon must find a way to reunite his family...

'Startlingly funny. Balances the gritty with the feel good' *Observer*

'A great read . . . harks back to the likes of Scout in *To Kill A Mockingbird*' Mariella Frostrup, BBC Radio 4

'A beautiful story told with compassion, urgency and wit' Stephen Kelman, author of the Booker-shortlisted *Pigeon English*

KIT DE WAAL

THE TRICK TO TIME

Birmingham, 1972. Mona is a young Irish girl in a big city, with the thrill of a new job and a room of her own in a busy boarding house. On her first night out in town, she meets William, a charming Irish boy with an easy smile and an open face. They embark upon a passionate love affair and a whirlwind marriage - before a sudden tragedy tears them apart.

Decades later, Mona pieces together the memories of the years that separate them. But can she ever learn to love again?

The Trick to Time is an unforgettable tale of grief, longing, and a love that lasts a lifetime.

'Authentic and beautiful, urgent and honest, this novel does what only the best do: it quietly makes room in your heart' - Chris Cleave on *My Name is Leon*

'Tender and heart-breaking' - Rachel Joyce on *My Name is Leon*

'A touching, thought-provoking debut' - *Guardian* on *My Name is Leon*

He just wanted a decent book to read ...

Not too much to ask, is it? It was in 1935 when Allen Lane, Managing Director of Bodley Head Publishers, stood on a platform at Exeter railway station looking for something good to read on his journey back to London. His choice was limited to popular magazines and poor-quality paperbacks – the same choice faced every day by the vast majority of readers, few of whom could afford hardbacks. Lane's disappointment and subsequent anger at the range of books generally available led him to found a company – and change the world.

'We believed in the existence in this country of a vast reading public for intelligent books at a low price, and staked everything on it'
Sir Allen Lane, 1902–1970, founder of Penguin Books

The quality paperback had arrived – and not just in bookshops. Lane was adamant that his Penguins should appear in chain stores and tobacconists, and should cost no more than a packet of cigarettes.

Reading habits (and cigarette prices) have changed since 1935, but Penguin still believes in publishing the best books for everybody to enjoy. We still believe that good design costs no more than bad design, and we still believe that quality books published passionately and responsibly make the world a better place.

So wherever you see the little bird – whether it's on a piece of prize-winning literary fiction or a celebrity autobiography, political tour de force or historical masterpiece, a serial-killer thriller, reference book, world classic or a piece of pure escapism – you can bet that it represents the very best that the genre has to offer.

Whatever you like to read – trust Penguin.